I0685103

The White Road to Verdun

Kathleen Burke

Contents

THE WHITE ROAD
TO VERDUN

BY

Kathleen Burke

This Little Book Is
Respectfully And Affectionately Dedicated To
Madame Jusserand,
Ambassadrice de France in Washington,
and to
Monsieur Gaston Liebert,
Consul General de France

Dr. C. O. Mailloux

And to all my good friends in the United States and Canada, whose sympathy and encouragement have helped me so much in my work.

VIVE LA FRANCE

The True Philosophers

We left Paris determined to undertake the journey to the Front in the true spirit of the French Poilu, and, no matter what happened, "de ne pas s'en faire." This famous "motto" of the French Army is probably derived from one of two slang sentences, de ne pas se faire des cheveux ("to keep one's hair on,") or de ne pas se faire de la bile, or, in other words, not to upset one's digestion by unnecessary worrying. The phrase is typical of the mentality of the Poilu, who accepts anything and everything that may happen, whether it be merely slight physical discomfort, or intense suffering, as part of the willing sacrifice which he made on the day that, leaving his homestead and his daily occupation, he took up arms "offering his body as a shield to defend the heart of France."

Everything might be worse than it is, says the Poilu, and so he has composed a Litany. Every regiment has a different version, but always with the same basis.

"Of two things one is certain: Either you're mobilised or you're not mobilised. If you're not mobilised, there is no need to worry; if you are mobilised, of two things one is certain: Either you're behind the lines or you're on the Front. If you're behind the lines there is no need to worry; if you're on the Front, of two things one is certain: Either you're resting in a safe place or you're exposed to danger. If you're resting in a safe place there is no need to worry; if you're exposed to danger, of two things one is certain: Either you're wounded or you're not wounded. If you're not wounded, there is no need to worry; if you are wounded, of two things one is certain: Either you're wounded seriously or you're wounded slightly. If you're wounded slightly there is no need to worry; if you're wounded seriously, of two things one is certain: Either you recover or you die. If you recover there is no need to worry; if you die you can't worry."

When once past the "Wall of China," as the French authorities call the difficult approaches to the war zone, Meaux was the first town of importance at which we stopped. We had an opportunity to sample the army bread, as the driver of a passing bread wagon flung a large round loaf into our motor.

According to all accounts received from the French soldiers who are in the prison camps of Germany, one of the greatest hardships is the lack of white bread, and they have employed various subterfuges in the endeavour to let their relatives know that they wish to have bread sent to them.

Some of the Bretons writing home nickname bread "Monsieur Barras," and when there was a very great shortage they would write to their families: "Ce pauvre Monsieur Barras ne se porte pas tres bien a present." (M. Barras is not very well at present.) Finally the Germans discovered the real significance of M. Barras and they added to one of the letters: "Si M. Barras ne se porte pas tres bien a present c'est bien la faute de vos amis les Anglais." (If M. Barras is not well at present, it is the fault of your friends the English.) And from then all the letters referring to M. Barras were strictly suppressed.

While the German Press may not be above admitting a shortage of food in Germany, it seriously annoys the Army that the French prisoners or the French in the invaded regions should hear of it. I heard one story of the wife of a French officer in Lille, who was obliged to offer unwilling hospitality to a German Captain, who, in a somewhat clumsy endeavour to be amiable, offered to try to get news of her husband and to convey it to her. Appreciating the seeming friendliness, of the Captain, she confided to him that she had means of communicating with her husband who was on the French Front. The Captain informed against her and the next day she was sent for by the Kommandantur, who imposed a fine of fifty francs upon her for having received a letter from the enemy lines. Taking a one hundred franc note from her bag she placed it on the desk, saying, "M. le Kommandantur, here is the fifty francs fine, and also another fifty francs which I am glad to subscribe for the starving women and children in Berlin." "No one starves in Berlin," replied the Kommandantur. "Oh, yes, they do," replied Madame X., "I know because the Captain who so kindly informed you that I had received a letter from my husband showed me a letter the other day from his wife in which she spoke of the sad condition of the women and children of Germany, who, whilst not starving, were far from happy." Thus she not only had the pleasure of seriously annoying the Kommandantur, but also had a chance to get even with the Captain who had informed against her, and who is no longer in soft quarters in Lille, but paying the penalty of his indiscretion by a sojourn on the Yser.

The Bridge At Meaux

The Bridge at Meaux, destroyed in the course of the German retreat, has not yet been entirely repaired. Beneath it rushes the Marne and the river sings in triumph, as it passes, that it is carrying away the soil that has been desecrated by the steps of the invader, and that day by day it is washing clean the land of France.

In the fields where the corn is standing, the tiny crosses marking the last resting places of the men are entirely hidden, but where the grain has been gathered the graves, stand out distinctly marked not only by a cross, but also by the tall bunches of corn which have been left growing on these small patches of holy ground. It has always been said that France has two harvests each year. Certainly in the fields of the Marne there is not only the harvest of bread; there is also springing up the harvest of security and peace.

The peasants as they point out the graves always add: "We of the people know that those men sacrificed their lives that our children might live. Those who have died in vain for an unjust cause may well envy the men of France who have poured out their blood for the benefit of humanity."

Looking on the crosses on the battlefield of the Marne, I realised to the fullest extent the sacrifices, borne with such bravery, of the women of France. I thought of the picture I had seen in Paris of a group of mothers standing at the foot of Calvary, looking out over the fields of small black crosses, lifting their hands to Heaven, with the words: "We also, God, have given our sons for the peace of the world."

At Montmirail the real activity of the war zone first became apparent. We drew the car to the side of the road and waited whilst a long procession of empty munition wagons passed on the way back from the munition parks near the fighting line. There was a smile on the face of every one of the drivers. Each of them had the satisfaction of knowing that there was no chance of his returning with an empty wagon, as there is no lack of provisions to feed the hungriest of the "75's" or any of her larger sisters.

The fact that it is known that there is an ample supply of munitions plays an important part in the "morale" of the troops. The average Poilu has no sympathy with the man who grumbles at the number of hours he may have to spend in the factory. We heard the tale of a munition worker who was complaining in a cafe at having to work so hard. A Poilu who was en permission, and who was sitting at the next table, turned to him saying: "You have no right to grumble. You receive ten to twelve francs a day for making shells and we poor devils get five sous a day for stopping them!"

Recruiting Rat-Catchers

We lunched in the small but hospitable village of Sezannes in company with a most charming invalided officer, who informed us that he was the principal in that district of the S.D.R. R.D. (Service de Recherche des Rattiers) (the Principal Recruiting Officer for Rat-Catchers). In other words, he is spending his time endeavouring to persuade suitable bow-wows to enlist in the service of their country. Likely dogs are trained until they do not bark, and become entirely accustomed to the sound of firing; they are then pronounced "aptes a faire campagne" or "fit for service," receive their livret militaire, or certificates--for not every chance dog is allowed in the trenches--and are despatched to the trenches on a rat-hunting campaign.

At the commencement of the .War, dogs were not utilized to the extent they are at present. A large number are now with the French Army and the wonderful training they have received, aided by their natural sagacity, renders them a holy terror to prowling bodies and spies. Those employed in carrying messages or tobacco to the soldiers in dangerous trenches now wear gas masks, as many of these high trained animals have been lost in consequence of too closely investigating the strange odour caused by this Hun war method.

From Sezannes we proceeded direct to the new camp for German prisoners at Connantre. The prisoners were mostly men who had been taken in the recent fighting on the Somme or around Verdun. The camp was already excellently installed and the prisoners were busy in groups gardening, making bread, or sitting before great heaps of potatoes preparing them for the evening meal. In one corner the inevitable German Band was preparing for an evening concert. The German sense of order was everywhere in evidence. In the long barracks where the men slept the beds were tidy, and above each bed was a small shelf, each shelf arranged in exactly the same order, the principal ornaments being a mug, fork and spoon; and just as each bed resembled each other bed, so the fork and spoon were placed in their respective mugs at exactly the same angle. There were small partitioned apartments for the non- commissioned officers.

The French Commander of the camp told us that the German love of holding some form of office was everywhere apparent. The French made no attempt to command the prisoners themselves, but always chose men from amongst the prisoners who were placed in authority over their comrades. The prisoners rejoiced exceedingly and promptly increased in self-importance and, alas, decreased in manners, if they were given the smallest position which raised them above the level of the rest of the men.

In the barrack where they were cutting up bread for the prisoners, we asked the men if they deeply regretted their captivity. They replied unanimously that they were "rather glad to be well fed," which seemed an answer in itself. They did not, however, appreciate the white bread, and stated that they preferred their own black bread. The French officers commanding the camp treat the prisoners as naughty children who must be "kept in the corner" and punished for their own good. In all my travels through France I have never seen any bitterness shown towards the prisoners. I remember once at Nevers we passed a group of German prisoners, and amongst them was a wounded man who was lying in a small cart. A hand bag had fallen across his leg, and none of his comrades attempted to remove it. A French woman pushing her way between the guards, lifted it off and gave it to one of the Germans to carry. When the guards tried to remonstrate she replied simply: "J'ai un fils prisonnier la bas, faut esperer qu'une allemande ferait autant pour lui." ("I have a son who is a prisoner in their land; let us hope that some German woman would do as much for him.")

On the battlefields the kindness of the French medical men to the German wounded has always been conspicuous. One of my neutral friends passing through Germany heard from one of the prominent German surgeons that they were well aware of this fact, and knew that their wounded received every attention. There is a story known throughout France of a French doctor who was attending a wounded German on the battlefield. The man, who was probably half delirious, snatched at a revolver which was lying near by and attempted to shoot the doctor. The doctor took the revolver from him, patted him on the head, and said: "Voyons, voyons, ne faites pas l'enfant" ("Now then, now then, don't be childish") and went on dressing his wounds.

Everywhere you hear accounts of brotherly love and religious tolerance. I remember kneeling once by the side of a dying French soldier who was tenderly supported in the arms of a famous young Mohammedan surgeon, an Egyptian who had taken his degree in Edinburgh and was now attached to the French Red Cross. The man's mind was wandering, and seeing a woman beside him he commenced to talk to me as to his betrothed. "This war cannot last always, little one, and when it is over we will buy a pig and a cow and we will go to the cure, won't we, beloved?" Then in a lucid moment he realised that he was dying, and he commenced to pray, "Ave Maria, Ave Maria," but the poor tired brain could remember nothing more. He turned to me to continue, but I could no longer trust myself to speak, and it was the Mohammedan who took up the prayer and continued it whilst the soldier followed with his lips until his soul passed away into the valley of shadows. I think this story is only equalled in its broad tolerance by that of the Rabbi Bloch of Lyons, who was shot at the battle of the Aisne whilst holding a crucifix to the lips of a dying Christian soldier. The soldier priests of France have earned the love and respect of even the most irreligious of the Poilus. They never hesitate to risk their lives, and have displayed sublime courage and devotion to their duty as priests and as soldiers. Behind the first line of trenches a soldier priest called suddenly to attend a dying comrade, took a small dog he was nursing and handing it to one of the men simply remarked, "Take care of the little beast for me, I am going to a dangerous corner and I do not want it killed."

A Gun Carriage An Altar

I have seen the Mass celebrated on a gun carriage. Vases made of shell cases were filled with flowers that the men had risked their lives to gather in order to deck the improvised altar. A Red Cross ambulance drove up and stopped near by. The wounded begged to be taken out on their stretchers and laid at the foot of the altar in order that "they might receive the blessing of the good God" before starting on the long journey to the hospital behind the lines.

Outside the prison camp of Cannantre stood a circle of French soldiers learning the bugle calls for the French Army. I wondered how the Germans cared to listen to the martial music of the men of France, one and all so sure of the ultimate victory of their country. Half a kilometre further on, a series of mock trenches had been made where the men were practising the throwing of hand grenades. Every available inch of space behind the French lines is made to serve some useful purpose.

I never see a hand grenade without thinking how difficult it is just now to be a hero in France. Every man is really a hero, and the men who have medals are almost ashamed since they know that nearly all their comrades merit them. It is especially difficult to be a hero in one's own family. One of the men in our hospital at Royaumont had been in the trenches during an attack. A grenade thrown by one of the French soldiers struck the parapet and rebounded amongst the men. With that rapidity of thought which is part of the French character, Jules sat on the grenade and extinguished it. For this act of bravery he was decorated by the French Government and wrote home to tell his wife. I found him sitting up in bed, gloomily reading her reply, and I enquired why he looked so glum. "Well, Mademoiselle," he replied, "I wrote to my wife to tell her of my new honour and see what she says: 'My dear Jules, We are not surprised you got a medal for sitting on a hand grenade; we have never known you to do anything else but sit down at home!!!'"

It was at Fere Champenoise that we passed through the first village which had been entirely destroyed by the retreating Germans. Only half the church was standing, but services are still held there every Sunday. Very little attempt has been made to rebuild the ruined houses. Were I one of the villagers I would prefer to raze to the ground all that remained of the desecrated homesteads and build afresh new dwellings; happy in the knowledge that with the victory of the Allies would start a period of absolute security, prosperity and peace.

Life Behind The Lines

Soon after leaving Mailly we had the privilege of beholding some of the four hundred centimetre guns of France, all prepared and ready to travel at a minute's notice along the railway lines to the section where they might be needed. Some idea of their size may be obtained from the fact that there were ten axles to the base on which they travel. They were all disguised by the system of camouflage employed by the French Army, and at a very short distance they blend with the landscape and become almost invisible. Each gun bears a different name, "Alsace," "Lorraine," etc., and with that strange irony and cynical wit of the French trooper, at the request of the men of one battery, one huge gun has been christened "Mosquito," "Because it stings."

The French often use a bitter and biting humour in speaking of the enemy. For instance, amongst the many pets of the men, the strangest I saw was a small hawk sitting on the wrist of a soldier who had trained him. The bird was the personification of evil. If any one approached he snapped at them and endeavoured to bite them. I asked the man why he kept him, and he replied that they had quite good sport in the trenches when they allowed the hawk to hunt small birds and field mice. Then his expression changing from jovial good humour to grimness, he added, "You know, I call him 'Zepp,' because he kills the little ones," (parcequ'il tue les tous petits.)

Devotion To Animals

In one small cantonment where two hundred Poilus sang, shouted, ate, drank and danced together to the strain of a wheezy gramophone, or in one word were "resting," I started to investigate the various kinds of pets owned by the troopers. Cats, dogs and monkeys were common, whilst one Poilu was the proud possessor of a parrot which he had purchased from a refugee obliged to fly from his home. He hastened to assure us that the bird had learned his "vocabulary" from his former proprietor. A study in black and white was a group of three or four white mice, nestling against the neck of a Senegalais.

The English Tommy is quite as devoted to animals as is his French brother. I remember crossing one bitter February day from Boulogne to Folkestone. Alongside the boat, on the quay at Boulogne, were lined up the men who had been granted leave. Arrayed in their shaggy fur coats they resembled little the smart British soldier of peace times. It was really wonderful how much the men managed to conceal under those fur coats, or else the eye of the officer inspecting them was intentionally not too keen.

Up the gangway trooped the men, and I noticed that two of them walked slowly and cautiously. The boat safely out of harbour, one of them produced from his chest a large tabby cat, whilst the other placed a fine cock on the deck. It was a cock with the true Gallic spirit, before the cat had time to consider the situation it had sprung on its back. The cat beat a hasty retreat into the arms of its protector who replaced it under his coat. Once in safety it stuck out its head and swore at the cock, which, perched on a coil of rope, crowed victoriously. Both had been the companions of the men in the trenches, and they were bringing them home.

A soldier standing near me began to grumble because he had not been able to bring his pet with him. I enquired why he had left it behind since the others had brought theirs away with them, and elicited the information that his pet was "a cow, and therefore somewhat difficult to transport." He seemed rather hurt that I should laugh, and assured me it was "a noble animal, brown with white spots, and had given himself and his comrades two quarts of milk a day." He looked disdainfully at the cock and cat. "They could have left them behind and no one would have pinched them, whereas I know I'll never see 'Sarah' again, she was far too useful."

Entering Vitry-le-Francois we had a splendid example of the typical "motto" of the French trooper, "Il ne faut pas s'en faire" One of the motor cars had broken down, and the officer-occupants, who were evidently not on an urgent mission, had gone to sleep on the banks by the side of the road whilst the chauffeur was making the necessary repairs. We offered him assistance, but he was progressing quite well alone. Later on another officer related to me his experience when his car broke down at midnight some twelve miles from a village. The chauffeur was making slow headway with the repairs. The officer enquired whether he really understood the job, and received the reply, "Yes, mon Lieutenant, I think I do, but I am rather a novice, as before the war I was a lion-tamer!" Apparently the gallant son of Gaul found it easier to tame lions than to repair motors.

Hunting For Generals

We left Vitry-le-Francois at six o'clock next morning, and started "the hunt for Generals." It is by no means easy to discover where the actual Headquarters of the General of any particular sector is situated.

We were not yet really on the "White Road" to Verdun, and there was still much to be seen that delighted the eyes. In one yellow cornfield there appeared to be enormous poppies. On approaching we discovered a detachment of Tirailleurs from Algiers, sitting in groups, and the "poppies" were the red fezes of the men--a gorgeous blending of crimson and gold. We threw a large box of cigarettes to them and were greeted with shouts of joy and thanks. The Tirailleurs are the enfants terribles of the French Army. One noble son of Africa who was being treated in one of the hospitals once presented me with an aluminium ring made from a piece of German shell. I asked him to make one for one of my comrades who was working at home, and he informed me that nothing would have given greater pleasure, but unfortunately he had no more aluminium. Later in the day, passing through the ward, I saw him surrounded by five or six Parisian ladies who were showering sweets, cigarettes and flowers on him, whilst he was responding by presenting each of them with an aluminium ring. When they had left I went to him and told him "Mahmud, that was not kind. I asked you for a ring and you said you had not got any more aluminium." He smiled and his nurse, who was passing, added, "No, he had not got any more aluminium, but when he is better he will get forty-eight hours' punishment; he has been into the kitchen, stolen one of our best aluminium saucepans, and has been making souvenirs for the ladies." He made no attempt to justify his action beyond stating: "Moi, pas si mauvais, toi pas faux souvenir" ("I am not so bad, I did not try to give you a fake souvenir").

Another of our chocolate coloured patients found in the grounds of the hospital an old umbrella. Its ribs stuck out and it was full of holes, but it gave him the idea of royalty and daily he sat up in bed in the ward with the umbrella unfurled whilst he laid down the law to his comrades. The nurses endeavoured to persuade him to hand it over at night. He obstinately refused, insisting that "he knew his comrades," and he feared that one of them would certainly steal the treasure, so he preferred to keep it in the bed with him.

At Villers-le-Sec we came upon the headquarters of the cooks for that section of the Front. The cook is one of the most important men in a French regiment; he serves many ends. When carrying the food through the communicating trenches to the front line trenches he is always supposed to bring to the men the latest news, the latest tale which is going the round of the camp, and anything that may happen to interest them. If he has not got any news he must manufacture and produce some kind of story. It is really necessary for him to be not only a cook but also an author.

There is a tale going the round of the French Army how one section of the Cooks, although unarmed, managed to take some twenty German prisoners. As they went on their way, they saw the Germans in the distance approaching them; the Head Cook quietly drew the field kitchens behind a clump of trees and bushes, placed his men in a row, each with a cooking utensil in his hand, and as the Germans passed shouted to them to surrender. The sun fell on the handles of the saucepans, causing them to shine like bayonets, and the Germans, taken unawares, laid down their arms. The Head Cook then stepped out and one by one took the rifles from the enemy and handed them to his men. It was only when he had disarmed the Germans and armed his comrades that he gave the signal for them to step out, and the Germans saw that they had been taken by a ruse. One can imagine the joy of the French troops in the next village when, with a soup ladle in his hand, his assistants armed with German rifles, followed by the soup kitchen and twenty prisoners--he marched in to report.

An Instance Of Quick Wit

It is curious how near humour is to tragedy in war, how quick wit may serve a useful purpose, and even save life. A young French medical student told me that he owed his life to the quick wit of the women of a village and the sense of humour of a Saxon officer. Whilst passing from one hospital to another he was captured by a small German patrol, and in spite of his papers proving that he was attached to the Red Cross Service, he was tried as a spy and condemned to be shot. At the opening of his trial the women had been interested spectators, towards the end all of them had vanished. He was placed against a barn door, the firing squad lined up, when from behind the hedge bordering a wood, the women began to bombard the soldiers with eggs. The aim was excellent, not one man escaped; the German officer laughed at the plight of his men and, in the brief respite accorded, the young man dashed towards the hedge and vanished in the undergrowth. The Germans fired a few shots but there was no organised attempt to follow him, probably because their own position was not too secure. He was loth to leave the women to face the music, but they insisted that it was pour la patrie and that they were quite capable of taking care of themselves. Later he again visited the village and the women told him that beyond obliging them to clean the soldiers' clothes thoroughly, the German officer had inflicted no other punishment upon them.

A certain number of inhabitants are still living in the village of Revigny. You see everywhere placards announcing "Caves pour 25," "Caves pour 100," and each person knows to which cellar he is to go if a Taube should start bombing the village. I saw one cellar marked "120 persons, specially safe, reserved for the children." Children are one of the most valuable assets of France, and a good old Territorial "Pe-Pere" (Daddy), as they are nicknamed, told me that it was his special but difficult duty to muster the children directly a Taube was signalled and chase them down into the cellar. Mopping his brow he assured me that it was not easy to catch the little beggars, who hid in the ruins, behind the army wagons, anywhere to escape the "parental" eye, even standing in rain barrels up to their necks in water. It is needless to add they consider it a grave infringement of their personal liberty and think that they should be allowed to remain in the open and see all that goes on, just as the little Londoners beg and coax to be allowed to stay up "to see the Zepps."

Passing the railway station we stopped to make some enquiries, and promptly ascertained all we wished to know from the Chef de Gare. In the days of peace there is in France no one more officious than the station master of a small but prosperous village. Now he is the meekest of men. Braided cap in hand he goes along the train from carriage door to carriage door humbly requesting newspapers for the wounded in the local hospitals: "Nous avons cent vingt cinq blesses ici, cela les fait tant de plaisir d'avoir des nouvelles." (We have 125 wounded here and they love to hear the news.)

In addition to levying a toll on printed matter, he casts a covetous and meaning glance on any fruit or chocolate that may be visible. Before the train is out of the station, you can see the once busy, and in his own opinion, all-important railway official, vanishing down the road to carry his spoils to his suffering comrades. Railway travelling is indeed expensive in France. No matter what time of day or night, wet or fine, the trains are met at each station by devoted women who extract contributions for the Red Cross Funds from the pockets of willing givers. It is only fair to state, however, that in most instances the station master gets there first.

At The Headquarters Of General Petain

From the time we left Revigny until we had passed into the Champagne country, upon the return journey from Verdun, we no longer saw a green tree or a blade of green grass; we were now indeed upon the "White Road which leads unto Verdun." Owing to an exceptionally trying and dry summer the roads are thick with white dust. The continual passing of the camions, the splendid transport wagons of the French Army, carrying either food, munitions, or troops, has stirred up the dust and coated the fields, trees and hedges with a thick layer of white. It is almost as painful to the eyes as the snow-fields of the Alps.

I saw one horse that looked exactly like a plaster statuette. His master had scrubbed him down, but before he dried the white dust had settled on him everywhere. Naturally humans do not escape. By the time our party reached the Headquarters of General Petain we had joined the White Brigade. I excused myself to the General, who smilingly replied: "Why complain, Mademoiselle, you are charming; your hair is powdered like that of a Marquise." The contrast with what had been a black fur cap on what was now perfectly white hair justified his compliment. I have never been renowned in my life for fear of any individual, but I must admit that I passed into the presence of General Petain with a great deal of respect amounting almost to awe. The defence of Verdun through the bitter months of February and March by General Petain, a defence which is now under the immediate control of his able lieutenants General Nivelle and General Dubois, has earned the respect and admiration of the whole world. It is impossible not to feel the deepest admiration for these men who have earned such undying glory, not only for themselves, but for their Motherland.

No one could have been more gracious and kind than General Petain, and in his presence one realised the strength and power of France. Throughout all the

French Headquarters one is impressed by the perfect calm; no excitement; everything perfectly organised.

General Petain asked me at once to tell him what I desired. I asked his permission to go to Rheims. He at once took up a paper which permitted me to enter the war zone and endorsed it with the request to General Debeney in Rheims to allow me to penetrate with my companions into the city. He then turned to me again and asked me, with a knowing smile, if that was all I required--for his Headquarters were hardly on the direct road to Rheims! I hesitated to express my real wish, when my good counsellor and friend, with whom I was making the journey, the Commandant Jean de Pulligny, answered for me: "I feel sure it would be a great happiness and honour if you would allow us, General, to go to Verdun." General Petain appeared slightly surprised, and turning to me asked: "Do you thoroughly realise the danger? You have crossed the Atlantic and faced submarines, but you will risk more in five minutes in Verdun than in crossing the Atlantic a thousand times." However, seeing that I was really anxious to go, and that it might be of great service to me in my future work to have seen personally the defence of Verdun, he added smilingly: "Well then, you can go if you wish at your own risk and peril." He then telephoned to General Nivelle the necessary permission for us to enter Verdun.

I doubt whether General Petain realises the respect in which he is held in all the civilised countries of the world. Probably he does not yet understand that people would come thousands of miles to have five minutes' audience with him, for he enquired if we were in any hurry to continue our journey, and added with charming simplicity--"Because if not, and you do not mind waiting an hour, I shall be glad if you will lunch with me."

A Meeting With "Forain"

We lunched with General Petain and his Etat Major. A charming and most interesting addition to the party was M. Forain, the famous French caricaturist, and now one of the Chief Instructors of the French Army in the art of camouflage--the art of making a thing look like anything in the world except what it is! He has established a series of schools all along the French Front, where the Poilus learn to bedeck their guns and thoroughly disguise them under delicate shades of green and yellow, with odd pink spots, in order to relieve the monotony. Certainly the appearance of the guns of the present time would rejoice the heart and soul of the "Futurists." It was most interesting to hear him describe the work in detail and the rapidity with which his pupils learned the new art. For one real battery there are probably three or four false ones, beautiful wooden guns, etc., etc., and he told us of the Poilus' new version of the song "Rien n'est plus beau que notre Patrie" ("Nothing is more beautiful than our country"). They now sing "Rien n'est plus faux que notre batterie" ("Nothing is more false than our battery").

It was M. Forain who coined the famous phrase "that there was no fear for the ultimate success of the Allies, if only the civilians held out!"

I was much amused at M. Forain's statement that he had already heard that a company had been formed for erecting, after the War, wooden hotels on the battle-fields of France for the accommodation of sightseers. Not only was it certain that these hotels were to be built, but the rooms were already booked in advance.

Value Of Women's Work

It was strange to find there, within the sound of the guns-- sometimes the glasses on the table danced to the music although no one took any notice of that--surrounded by men directing the operations of the war and of one of the greatest battles in history, how little War was mentioned. Science, Philosophy and the work of women were discussed.

The men of France are taking deep interest in the splendid manner in which the women of all the different nations are responding to the call to service. I described to General Petain the work of the Scottish Women's Hospitals. These magnificent hospitals are organised and staffed entirely by women and started, in the first instance, by the Scottish Branch of the National Union of Women's Suffrage. He was deeply interested to learn that what had been before the War a political society had, with that splendid spirit of patriotism which had from the first day of the war animated every man, woman and child of Great Britain, drawn upon its funds and founded the Hospital Units. I explained to him that it was no longer a question of politics, but simply a case of serving humanity and serving it to the best possible advantage. The National Union had realised that this was a time for organised effort on the part of all women for the benefit of the human race and the alleviation of suffering.

I spoke of the bravery of our girls in Serbia; how many of them had laid down their lives during the typhus epidemic; how cheerfully they had borne hardships, our doctors writing home that their tent hospitals were like "great white birds spreading their wings under the trees," whereas really they had often been up all night hanging on to the tent poles to prevent the tents collapsing over their patients.

A member of the Etat Major asked how we overcame the language difficulty.

I pointed out that to diagnose typhus and watch the progress of the patient it was not necessary to speak to him, and that by the magic language of sympathy we managed to establish some form of "understanding" between the patients, the Doctors, and the Nurses. The members of our staff were chosen as far as possible with a knowledge of French or German, and it was possible to find many Serbians speaking either one of these languages. We also found interpreters amongst the Austrian prisoner orderlies. These prisoner orderlies had really proved useful and had done their best to help us. Naturally they had their faults. One of our Lady Doctors had as orderly a Viennese Professor, willing but somewhat absent-minded. One morning she sent for him and asked him: "Herr Karl, can you tell me what was wrong with my bath water this morning?" "I really don't know, Fraulein, but I will endeavour to find out."

Ten minutes later he returned, looking decidedly guilty and stammered out, "I do not know how to tell you what happened to that bath water." "Nonsense, it can't be very terrible," replied Doctor X. "What was wrong?" "Well, Fraulein, when I went into the camp kitchen this morning there were two cauldrons there, one was your bath water, and the other was the camp soup. To you, Fraulein, I brought the camp soup."

We who had worked with the Serbians had learned to respect and admire them for their patriotism, courage and patient endurance. We felt that their outstanding characteristic was their imagination, which, turned into the proper channels and given a chance to develop, should produce for the world not only famous painters and poets but also great inventors. This vivid imagination is found in the highest and lowest of the land. To illustrate it, I told my neighbour at table a tale related to me by my good friend Dr. Popovic. "Two weary, ragged Serbian soldiers were sitting huddled together waiting to be ordered forward to fight. One asked the other, 'Do you know how this War started, Milan? You don't. Well then I'll tell you. The Sultan of Turkey sent our King Peter a sack of rice. King Peter looked at the sack, smiled, then took a very small bag and went into his garden and filled it with red pepper. He sent the bag of red pepper to the Sultan of Turkey. Now, Milan, you can see what that meant. The Sultan of Turkey said to our Peter, 'My army is as numerous as the grains of rice in this sack,' and by sending a small bag of red pepper to the Sultan our Peter replied, 'My Army is not very numerous, but it is mighty hot stuff.'"

Many members of the Units of the Scottish Women's Hospitals who had been driven out of Serbia at the time of the great invasion had asked to be allowed to return to work for the Serbians, and we were now equipping fresh units, entirely staffed by women, to serve with the Serbian Army, besides having at the present time the medical care of six thousand Serbian refugees on the island of Corsica.

General Petain said smiling that before the war he had sometimes thought of women "as those who inspired the most beautiful ideas in men and prevented them from carrying them out," but the war, he added, had certainly proved conclusively the value of women's work.

M. Forain expressed the desire to visit the chief French Hospital of the Scottish Women at the Abbaye de Royaumont. The General laughingly told him, "You do not realise how stern and devoted to duty those ladies are. I wonder if you would be permitted to visit them?"

I consoled M. Forain by pointing out that surely as chief Camoufler (disguiser) of the French Army, he could disguise himself as a model of virtue (de se cam-oufler en bon garcon). Certainly this son of France, who has turned his brilliant intellect and his art to the saving of men's lives, would be welcome anywhere and everywhere. I hastened to assure him that I was only teasing him, and added that I only teased the people I admired and liked. General Petain immediately turned to the Commandant de Pulligny--"Please remark that she has not yet teased me." "Probably because she fears to do it, and has too much respect for you," replied the Commandant. "Fears! I do not think we need talk of that just now, when she dares to go to Verdun."

Whilst at coffee after lunch the news came of the continued advance of the British troops. General Petain turned to me and said, "You must indeed be proud in England of your new army. Please tell your English people of our admiration of the magnificent effort of England. The raising and equipping of your giant army in such a short time was indeed a colossal task. How well it was carried out all the world now knows and we are reaping the harvest."

The General's Chief of Staff added: "Lord Kitchener was right when he said the war would last three years"--"the first year preparation, the second year defence, and the third year cela sera rigolo (it will be huge sport)." He quoted the phrase as

Lord Kitchener's own.

Before we left the General signed for me the menu of the lunch, pointing out to me, however, that if I were at any time to show the menu to the village policeman I must assure him that the hare which figured thereon had been run over at night by a motor car and lost its life owing to an accident, otherwise he might, he feared, be fined for killing game out of season!

I shall always remember the picture of General Petain seeing us into our car with his parting words, "You are about to do the most dangerous thing you have ever done or will ever do in your life. As for Verdun, tell them in England that I am smiling and I am sure that when you see General Nivelle you will find him smiling too. That is the best answer I can give you as to how things are going with us at Verdun." Then with a friendly wave of his hand we passed on our way.

After leaving the Headquarters of General Petain we were held up for some time at a level crossing and watched the busy little train puffing along, carrying towards Verdun stores, munitions and men. This level crossing had been the scene of active fighting; on each side were numerous graves, and the sentinels off duty were passing from one to the other picking a dead leaf or drawing a branch of trailing vine over the resting places of their comrades.

Above our heads circled "les guipes" the wasps of the French Army. They had been aroused by the appearance of a Taube and were preparing to sting had the Taube waited or made any further attempt to proceed over the French lines. However, deciding that discretion was the better part of valour, it turned and fled.

It is unwise, however, to stir up the "wasps of France"; they followed it, and later in the day we heard that it had been brought down near Verdun.

We were now in the centre of activity of the army defending Verdun. On every hand we saw artillery parks, ammunition parks, and regiments resting, whilst along the road a long line of camions passed unceasingly. During the whole length of my stay on the French Front I only saw one regiment marching. Everywhere the men are conveyed in the camions, and are thus spared the fatigue which would otherwise be caused by the intense heat and the white dust. There are perhaps only two things that can in any way upset the perfect indifference to difficulties of the French trooper: he hates to walk, and he refuses to be deprived of his "pinard." The men of the French Army have named their red wine "pinard," just as they call water "la flotte," always, however, being careful to add that "la flotte" is excellent "for washing one's feet."

As we passed through the Headquarters of General Nivelle, he sent down word to us not to wait to call on him then, but to proceed at once to Verdun as later the passage would become more difficult. He kindly sent down to us one of the officers of his staff to act as escort. The officer sat by our chauffeur, warning him of the' dangerous spots in the road which the Germans had the habit of "watering" from time to time with "marmites," and ordering him to put on extra speed. Our speed along the road into Verdun averaged well over a mile a minute.

The "Movies" Under Fire

Within range of the German guns, probably not more than four or five kilometres from Verdun, we came on a line of men waiting their turn to go into the cinema. After all there was no reason "de s'en faire," and if they were alive they decided they might as well be happy and amused. Just before entering the gate of Verdun we passed a number of ambulances, some of them driven by the American volunteers. These young Americans have displayed splendid heroism in bringing in the wounded under difficult conditions. Many of them have been mentioned in despatches, and have received from France the Croix de Guerre. I also saw an ambulance marked "Lloyds."

It would be useless to pretend that one entered Verdun without emotion,-- Verdun, sorely stricken, yet living, kept alive by the indomitable soul of the soldiers of France, whilst her wounds are daily treated and healed by the skill of her Generals. A white city of desolation, scorched and battered, yet the brightest jewel in the crown of France's glory; a shining example to the world of the triumph of human resistance and the courage of men. A city of strange and cruel sounds. The short, sharp bark of the 75's, the boom of the death-dealing enemy guns, the shrieks of the shells and the fall of masonry parting from houses to which it had been attached for centuries, whilst from the shattered window frames the familiar sprite of the household looked ever for the children who came no longer across the thresholds of the homes. Verdun is no longer a refuge for all that is good and beautiful and tender, and so the sounds of the voices of children and of birds are heard no more. Both have flown; the children were evacuated with the civilians in the bitter months of February and March, and the birds, realising that there is no secure place in which to nest, have deserted not only Verdun but the whole of the surrounding district.

We proceeded to a terrace overlooking the lower part of the town and witnessed a duel between the French and German artillery. The Germans were bombarding the barracks of Chevert, and from all around the French guns were replying. It was certainly a joy to note that for one boom of a German cannon there were certainly ten answers from the French guns. The French soldiers off duty should have been resting in the caves and dug-outs which have been prepared for them, but most of them were out on the terraces in different parts of the city, smoking and casually watching the effect of the German or of their own fire. I enquired of one Poilu whether he would be glad to leave Verdun, and he laughingly replied: "One might be worse off than here. This is the time of year that in peace times I should have been staying in the country with my mother-in-law."

There is no talk of peace in Verdun. I asked one of the men when he thought the war would end. "Perfectly simple to reply to that, Mademoiselle; the war will end the day that hostilities cease."

I believe that the Germans would not be sorry to abandon the siege of Verdun. In one of the French newspapers I saw the following verse:

Boches, a l'univers votre zele importun Fait des "communiques" dont personne n'est dupe. Vous dites: "Nos soldats occuperont Verdun. Jusqu'ici c'est plutot Verdun qui les occupe."

(You say that you soon will hold Verdun, Whilst really Verdun holds you.)

We left the car and climbed through the ruined streets to the top of the citadel. No attempt has been made to remove any of the furniture or effects from the demolished houses. In those houses from which only the front had been blown away the spoons and forks were in some instances still on the table, set ready for the meal that had been interrupted.

From windows lace curtains and draperies hung out over the fronts of the houses. Everywhere shattered doors, broken cupboards, drawers thrown open where the inhabitants had thought to try to save some of their cherished belongings, but had finally fled leaving all to the care of the soldiers, who protect the property of the inhabitants as carefully as if it were their own.

It would be difficult to find finer custodians. I was told that at Bobigny, pres Bourget, there is on one of the houses the following inscription worthy of classical times:

"The proprietor of this house has gone to the War. He leaves this dwelling to the care of the French. Long live France." And he left the key in the lock.

The soldiers billeted in the house read the inscription, which met with their approval, and so far each regiment in passing had cleaned out the little dwelling and left it in perfect order.

From the citadel we went down into the trenches which led to the lines at Thiaumont. The heat in the city was excessive but in the trenches it was delightfully cool, perhaps a little too cool. We heard the men make no complaints except that at times the life was a little "monotonous"! One man told me that he was once in a trench that was occupied at the same time by the French and the Germans. There was nothing between them but sand bags and a thick wall of clay, and day and night the French watched that wall. One day a slight scratching was heard. The men prepared to face the crumbling of the barrier when through a small hole popped out the head of a brown rabbit. Down into the trench hopped Mrs. Bunny, followed by two small bunnies, and although rabbit for lunch would have improved the menu the men had not the heart to kill her. On the contrary they fed her on their rations and at night- fall she departed, followed by her progeny.

From all the dug-outs heads popped out and the first movement of surprise at seeing a woman in the trenches turned to a smile of delight, since the Poilu is at all times a chivalrous gentleman. One man was telling me of the magnificent work that had been accomplished by his "compagnie." I congratulated him and told him he must be happy to be in such a company. He swept off his iron casque, bowed almost to the ground, and answered: "Certainly I am happy in my company, Mademoiselle, but I am far happier in yours." The principal grief of the Poilus appeared to be that a shell two or three days before had destroyed the store of the great "dragee" (sugared almond) manufactory of Verdun. Before leaving the manufacturer had bequeathed his stock to the Army and they were all regretting that they had not been greedier and eaten up the "dragees" quicker.

In the trenches near Verdun, as in the trenches in Flanders, you find the men talking little of war, but much of their homes and their families. I came once upon a group of Bretons. They had opened some tins of sardines and sitting around a bucket of blazing coals they were toasting the fish on the ends of small twigs. I asked them why they were wasting their energies since the fish were ready to be eaten straight from the tins. "We know," they replied, "but it smells like home." I suppose with the odour of the cooking fish, in the blue haze of the smoke, they saw visions of their cottages and the white-coiffed Bretonnes frying the fresh sardines that they had caught.

The dusk was now falling and, entering the car, we proceeded towards the lower part of the town at a snail's pace in order not to draw the German fire. We were told that at the present time approximately one hundred shells a day still fall on Verdun, but at the time of the great attack the number was as high as eight hundred, whilst as many as two hundred thousand shells fell daily in and around Verdun.

Just before we reached the entrance to the citadel the enemy began to shell the city and one of the shells exploded within two hundred feet of the car. We knew that we were near the entrance to the vaults of the citadel and could take refuge, so we left the car and proceeded on foot. Without thinking we walked in the centre of the road, and the sentinel at the door of the citadel began in somewhat emphatic French to recommend us to "longer les murs" (to hug the walls tightly). The Germans are well aware of the entrance to the citadel and daily shell the spot. If one meets a shell in the centre of the road it is obviously no use to argue, whilst in hugging the side of the wall there is a possibility of only receiving the fragments of the bursting shell.

A Subterranean City

The subterranean galleries of the citadel of Verdun were constructed by Vauban, and are now a hive of activity--barbers' shops, sweet shops, boot shops, hospitals, anything and. everything which goes to make up a small city.

One of the young officers placed his "cell" at our disposal. The long galleries are all equipped with central heating and electric light and some of them have been divided off by wooden partitions or curtains like the dormitories in a large school. In the "cell" allocated to us we could see the loving touch of a woman's hand. Around the pillow on the small camp bed was a beautiful edging of Irish lace, and on the dressing-table a large bottle of Eau-de-Cologne. There is no reason to be too uncomfortable in Verdun when one has a good little wife to think of one and to send presents from time to time.

Emerging from the galleries we met General Dubois, a great soldier and a kindly man, one who shares the daily perils of his men. The General invited us to remain and dine with him. He had that day received from General Nivelle his "cravate" as Commander of the Legion of Honour, and his officers were giving him a dinner-party to celebrate the event. "See how kind fate is to me," he added; "only one thing was missing from the feast--the presence of the ladies--and here you are."

It would need the brush of Rembrandt to paint the dining-hall in the citadel of Verdun. At one long table in the dimly lighted vault sat between eighty and ninety officers, who all rose, saluted, and cheered as we entered. The General sat at the head of the table surrounded by his staff, and behind him the faces of the cooks were lit up by the fires of the stoves.

Some short distance behind us was an air-shaft. It appears that about a week or a fortnight before our arrival a German shell, striking the top part of the citadel, dislodged some dust and gravel which fell down the air-shaft onto the General's head. He simply called the attendants to him and asked for his table to be moved forward a yard, as he did not feel inclined to sit at table with his helmet on.

An excellent dinner--soup, roast mutton, fresh beans, salade Russe, Frangipane, dessert--and even champagne to celebrate the General's cravate--quite reassured us that people may die in Verdun of shells but not of hunger. We drank toasts to France, the Allies, and, silently, to the men of France who had died that we might live. I was asked to propose the health of the General and did it in English, knowing that he spoke English well. I told him that the defenders of Verdun would live in our hearts and memories; that on behalf of the whole British race I felt I might convey to him congratulations on the honour paid to him by France. I assured him that we had but one idea and one hope, the speedy victory of the Allied arms, and that personally my present desire was that every one of those present at table might live to see the flag of France waving over the whole of Alsace-Lorraine. They asked me to repeat a description of the flag of France which I gave first in Ottawa, so there, in the citadel of Verdun with a small French flag before me, I went back in spirit to Ottawa and remembered how I had spoken of the triumph of the flag of France: "The red, white and blue--the red of the flag of France a little deeper hue than in time of peace since it was dyed with the blood of her sons, the blood in which a new history of France is being written, volume on volume, page on page, of deeds of heroism, some pages completed and signed, others where the pen has dropped from the faltering hands and which posterity must needs finish. The white of the flag of France, not quite so white as in time of peace since thousands of her sons had taken it in their hands and pressed it to their lips before they went forward to die for it, yet without stain, since in all the record of the war there is no blot on the escutcheon of France. And the blue of the flag of France, true blue, torn and tattered with the marks of the bullets and the shrapnel, yet unfurling proudly in the breeze whilst the very holes were patched by the blue of the sky, since surely Heaven stands behind the flag of France."

The men of Verdun were full of admiration for the glorious Commander of the Fort de Vaux. They told me that the fort was held, or rather the ruins of the fort, until the Germans were actually on the top and firing on the French beneath.

I discussed with my neighbour the fact that the Germans had more hatred for us than for the French. He said the whole world would ridicule the Germans for the manner in which they had exploited the phrase "Gott strafe England," writing it even on the walls anywhere and everywhere. He added laughingly that it should not worry the English comrades. "When they read 'Gott strafe England' all they needed to reply was 'Ypres, Ypres, Hurrah!'"

Poilu And Tommy

He informed me that he had been stationed for some time with his regiment near the English troops, and there had been loud lamentations among the Poilus because they had been obliged to say good-bye to their English comrades. He added that the affection was not entirely disinterested. The English comrades had excellent marmalade and jam and other good things which they shared with their French brothers, who, whilst excellently fed, do not indulge in these luxuries. He told me a delightful tale of a French cook who, seeing an English soldier standing by, began to question him as to his particular branch of the service, informing him that he himself had had an exceedingly busy morning peeling potatoes and cleaning up the pots and pans. After considerable conversation he inquired of the English comrade what he did for his living. "Oh," replied the Englishman, "I get my living fairly easily; nothing half so strenuous as peeling potatoes. I am just a colonel."!!

The clean-shaven Tommy is the beloved of all France. I remember seeing one gallant khaki knight carrying the market basket of a French maiden and repaying himself out of her store of apples. I regret to say his pockets bulged suspiciously. Whilst at a level crossing near by, the old lady in charge of the gate had an escort of "Tommies" who urged her to let the train "rip." This was somewhat ironical in view of the fact that the top speed in that part of the war zone was probably never more than ten miles an hour.

Tommy is never alone The children have learned that he loves their company and he is always surrounded by an escort of youthful admirers. The children like to rummage in his pockets for souvenirs: he must spend quite a good deal of his pay purchasing sweets so that they may not be disappointed and that there may be something for his little friends to find. I remember seeing one Tommy, sitting in the dusty road with a large pot of marmalade between his legs, dealing out spoonfuls with perfect justice and impartiality to a circle of youngsters. He speaks to them of his own little "nippers" at home and they in turn tell him of their father who is fighting, of their mother who now works in the fields, and of baby who is fearfully ignorant, does not know the difference between the French and the "Engleesch" and who insisted on calling the great English General who had stayed at their farm "Papa." It matters little that they cannot understand each other, and it does not in the least prevent them from holding lengthy conversations.

I told my companion at table that whilst visiting one of the hospitals in France I had heard how one Englishman had been sent into a far hospital in Provence by mistake. He was not seriously injured and promptly constituted himself king of the ward. On arrival he insisted on being shaved. As no shaving brush was available the "piou-piou" in the next bed lathered him with his tooth brush. The French cooking did not appeal to him, and he grumbled continuously. The directress of the hospital sent her own cook from her chateau to cater for Mr. Atkins. An elaborate menu was prepared. Tommy glanced through it, ordered everything to be removed, and commanded tea and toast. Toast-making is not a French art and the chateau chef was obliged to remain at the hospital and spend his time carefully preparing the toast and seeing that it was served in good condition. When Mr. Atkins felt so disposed he would summon a piou-piou to give him a French lesson or else request the various inmates of the ward to sing to him. He would in turn render that plaintive ditty, "Down by the Old Bull and Bush." A nurse who spoke a little English translated his song to the French soldiers! Whilst not desiring to criticise the rendez-vous selected by their "camerade anglais," they did not consider that "pres d'un vieux taureau" (near an old bull) was a safe or desirable meeting-place. When I explained to the nurse that "The Bull and Bush" was a kind of cabaret she hastened from ward to ward to tell the men that after all the Englishman might have selected a worse spot to entertain his girl. He was at once the joy and the despair of the whole hospital and the nurse had much trouble in consoling the patients when "our English" was removed.

Abbreviated French

When Tommy indulges in the use of the French language he abbreviates it as much as possible.

One hot summer's day driving from Boulogne to Fort Mahon, half way down a steep hill we came upon two Tommies endeavouring to extract a motor cycle and a side-car from a somewhat difficult position. They had side-slipped and run into a small tree. The cycle was on one side and the side-car on the other, and a steel rod between had been rammed right into the wood through the force of the collision.

My three companions and myself endeavoured to help the men to pull out the rod, but the united efforts of the six of us proved unavailing. We hailed a passing cart and tied the reins around the motor-cycle, but immediately the horse commenced to pull the leather of the reins snapped. Behind the cart walked a peasant. Only one adjective can possibly describe him: he was decidedly "beer-y." He made no attempt to help but passed from one Tommy to the other, patting them on their backs, assuring them "that with a little good-will all would be well." There was a dangerous glint in the youngest Tommy's eye, but in the presence of ladies he refrained from putting his thoughts into words. Finally, his patience evaporating, he suddenly turned on the peasant and shouted at him, "Ong! Ong!" It took me some time to grasp that this was Tommy's abbreviated version of "Allez vous en" (Clear out). In any event it proved quite useless, as he continued to pat the Tommies affectionately and to bombard them with impracticable suggestions.

We were joined later by three villagers, two gendarmes and a postman, and, all pulling together, we managed to extract the rod from the tree. A large lorry was passing and on to it we heaved the wreckage. Up clambered the Tommies, followed by their unwelcome friend, who managed to sit on the only unbroken portion of the side-car. This was too much for Messrs. Atkins' equanimity. Limp with laughter, we watched them pass from sight amidst a chorus of "Ong! Ong!" followed by flights of oratory in the English tongue which do not bear repeating, but which were received by the peasant as expressions of deep esteem and to which he replied by endeavouring to kiss the Tommies and shouting, "Vive l'Angleterre! All right! Hoorah!"

Our guiding officer began to show some signs of anxiety to have us leave before ten o'clock, but the good-byes took some time. Presents were showered upon us, German dragees (shell heads and pieces of shrapnel), and the real French dragees, the famous sweet of Verdun.

We crept out of the city, but unfortunately at one of the dangerous crossroads our chauffeur mistook the route. A heavy bombardment was taking place and the French were replying. We were lucky enough to get on to the route and into safety before any shell fell near us. It appears that the Germans systematically bombard the roads at night, hoping to destroy the camions bringing up the food for the city, fresh munitions and men.

We slept that night at Bar-le-Duc, and next morning saw the various ambulances and hospitals which the Service de Sante had particularly requested me to visit. I was impressed by the splendid organisation of the Red Cross even quite close to the firing line.

The Brown And Black Sons Of France

Passing through one tent hospital an Algerian called out to me: "Ohe, la blonde, viens ici! J'ai quelque chose de beau a te montrer." (Come here, fair girl, I have something pretty to show you.) He was sitting up in bed, and, as I approached, unbuttoned his bed-jacket and insisted on my examining the tag of his vest on which was written, "Leader, London." The vest had come in a parcel of goods from the London Committee of the French Red Cross, and I only wished that the angel of goodness and tenderness, who is the Presidente of the Croix Rouge, Mme. de la Panouse, and that Mr. D. H. Illingworth, Mr. Philip Wilkins, and all her able lieutenants, could have seen the pleasure on the face of this swarthy defender of France. In the next bed was a Senegalais who endeavoured to attract my attention by keeping up a running compliment to my compatriots, my King, and myself. He must have chanted fifty times: "Vive les English, Georges, et toi!" He continued even after I had rewarded him with some cigarettes. The Senegalais and the Algerians are really great children, especially when they are wounded. I have seen convalescent Senegalais and Algerians in Paris spend hours in the Champs Elysees watching the entertainment at the open-air marionette theatre. The antics of the dolls kept them amused. They are admitted to the enclosure free, and there is no longer any room for the children who frequented the show in happier days. These latter form a disconsolate circle on the outside, whilst the younger ones, who do not suffer from colour prejudice, scramble onto the knees of the black soldiers.

The sister in charge was a true daughter of the "Lady of the Lamp." Provided they are really ill, she sympathises with all the grumblers, but scolds them if they have reached the convalescent stage. She carries a small book in which she enters imaginary good points to those who have the tables by their beds tidy, and she pinned an invisible medal on the chest of a convalescent who was helping to carry trays of food to his comrades. She is indeed a General, saving men for France.

Not a man escaped her attention, and as we passed through the tents she gave to each of her "chers enfants," black or white, a cheering smile or a kindly word. She did, however, whilst talking to us, omit to salute a Senegalais. Before she passed out of the tent he commenced to call after her, "Toi pas gentille aujourd'hui, moi battre toi." (You are not good to me to-day; me beat you.) This, it appears, is his little joke--he will never beat any one again, since he lost both his arms when his trench was blown up by a land mine.

It was at Triancourt that I first saw in operation the motor-cars that had been sent out fitted with bath tubs for the troops, and also a very fine car fitted up by the London Committee of the French Red Cross as a moving dental hospital.

I regret to add that a "Poilu" near by disrespectfully referred to it as "another of the horrors of war," adding that in times of peace there was some kind of personal liberty, whereas now "a man could not have toothache without being forced to have it ended, and that there was no possibility of escaping a dentist who hunted you down by motor."

It was suggested that as I had had a touch of toothache the night before, I might take my place in the chair and give an example of British pluck to the assembled "Poilus." I hastened to impress on the surgeon that I hated notoriety and would prefer to remain modestly in the background. I even pushed aside with scorn the proffered bribe of six "Boche," buttons, assuring the man that "I would keep my toothache as a souvenir."

At one of the hospitals beside the bed of a dying man sat a little old man writing letters. They told me that before the war he had owned the most flourishing wine shop in the village. He had fled before the approach of the German troops, but later returned to his village and installed himself in the hospital as scribe. He wrote from morning until night, and, watching him stretching his lean old hands, I asked him if he suffered much pain from writers' cramp. He looked at me almost reproachfully before answering, "Mademoiselle, it is the least I can do for my country; besides my pain is so slight and that of the comrades so great. I am proud, indeed proud, that at sixty-seven years of age I am not useless."

I was shown a copy of the last letter dictated by a young French officer, and I asked to be allowed to copy it--it was indeed a letter of a "chic" type.

Chers Parrain et Marraine,

Je vous ecris a vous pour ne pas tuer Maman qu'un pareil coup surprendrait trop.

J'ai ete blesse le ... devant ... J'ai deux blessures hideuses et je n'en aurai pas pour bien longtemps. Les majors ne me le cachent meme pas.

Je pars sans regret avec la conscience d'avoir fait mon devoir.

Prevenez done mes parents le mieux que vous pourrez; qu'ils ne cherchent pas a venir, ils n'en auraient pas le temps.

Adieu vous tous que j'aimais.

VIVE LA FRANCE!

Dear Godfather and Godmother,

I am writing to you so as not to kill Mother, whom such a shock would surprise too much. I was wounded on the ... at ... I have two terrible wounds and I cannot last long. The surgeons do not even attempt to conceal this from me. I go without regret, with the consciousness of having done my duty. Kindly break the news to my parents the best way you can; they should not attempt to come because they would not have time to reach me before the end.

Farewell to all you whom I have loved.

LONG LIVE FRANCE!

Whilst loving his relatives tenderly, the last thought of the dying Frenchman is for his country. Each one dies as a hero, yet not one realises it. It would be impossible to show greater simplicity; they salute the flag for the last time and that is all.

At General Nivelle's Headquarters

From Triancourt we went straight to the Headquarters of General Nivelle. They had just brought him the maps rectified to mark the French advance. The advance had been made whilst we were standing on the terrace at Verdun the night before. We had seen the rockets sent up, requesting a "tir de barrage" (curtain of fire). The 75's had replied at once and the French had been able to carry out the operation.

Good news had also come in from the Somme, and General Nivelle did not hesitate to express his admiration for the British soldiers.

He said that there was no need to praise the first troops sent by Britain to France, every one knew their value, but it should be a great satisfaction to Britain to find that the new army was living up to the traditions of the old army.

He added: "We can describe the new Army of Britain in two words: Ca mord--it bites."

The Father of his own men, it is not surprising that General Nivelle finds a warm corner in his heart for the British Tommy, since his Mother was an Englishwoman.

At lunch General Nivelle and the members of his staff asked many questions as to the work of the Scottish Women's Hospitals. I told them that what appealed to us most in our French patients was the perfect discipline and the gratitude of the men. We are all women in the Hospitals, and the men might take advantage of this fact to show want of discipline, but we never had to complain of lack of obedience. These soldiers of France may some of them before the war have been just rough peasants, eating, drinking, and sleeping; even having thoughts not akin to knighthood, but now, through the ordeal of blood and fire, each one of them has won his spurs and come out a chivalrous knight, and they bring their chivalry right into the hospitals with them. We had also learned to love them for their kindness to one another. When new wounded are brought in and the lights are low in the hospital wards, cautiously watching if the Nurse is looking (luckily Nurses have a way of not seeing everything), one of the convalescents will creep from his bed to the side of the new arrival and ask the inevitable question: "D'ou viens-tu?" (Where do you come from?) "I come from Toulouse," replies the man. "Ah," says the enquirer, "my wife's Grandmother had a cousin who lived near Toulouse." That is quite a sufficient basis for a friendship. The convalescent sits by the bedside of his new comrade, holding the man's hand, whilst his wounds are being dressed, telling him he knows of the pain, that he, too, has suffered, and that soon all will be well.

Lions to fight, ever ready to answer to the call of the defence of their country, yet these men of France are tender and gentle. In one hospital through which I passed there was a baby. It was a military hospital, and no civilian had any right there, but the medical officers who inspected the hospital were remarkably blind --none of them could ever see the baby. One of the soldiers passing through a bombarded village saw a little body lying in the mud, and although he believed the child to be dead he stooped down and picked it up. At the evacuating station the baby and the soldier were sent to the hospital together; the doctors operated upon the baby and took a piece of shrapnel from its back, and, once well and strong, it constituted itself lord and master and king of all it surveyed. When it woke in the morning it would call "Papa" and twenty fathers answered to its call. All the pent-up love of the men for their own little ones from whom they had been parted for so long they lavished on the tiny stranger, but all his affection and his whole heart belonged to the rough miner soldier who had brought him in. As the shadows fell one saw the man walking up and down the ward with the child in his arms, crooning the "Marseillaise" until the tired little eyes closed. He had obtained permission from the authorities to adopt the child as the parents could not be found, and remarked humorously: "Mademoiselle, it is so convenient to have a family without the trouble of being married!"

What we must remember is that the rough soldier, himself blinded with blood and mud, uncertain whether he could ever reach a point of safety, yet had time to stoop and pick that little flower of France and save it from being crushed beneath the cannon wheels. I told General Nivelle that the hospital staff intended to keep the child for the soldier until the end of the war, and we all hoped that he might grow up to the glory of France and to the eternal honour of the tender-hearted fighter who had rescued him.

After lunch we stood for some time watching the unending stream of camions proceeding into Verdun. I believe it has been stated that on the average one passed through the village every fifteen seconds, and that there are something like twelve thousand motor vehicles used in the defence of Verdun. The splendid condition of the roads and the absence of all confusion in the handling of this immense volume of traffic are a great tribute to the organising genius of the chiefs of the French Army.

We left General Nivelle as General Petain predicted we should find him--smiling.

Rheims

We slept that night at Epernay, in the heart of the Champagne district. The soil of France is doing its best to keep the vines in perfect condition and to provide a good vintage to be drunk later to celebrate the victory of France and her Allies. The keeping of the roads in good condition is necessary for the rapid carrying out of operations on the Front, and a "marmite" hole is promptly filled if by a lucky shot the German batteries happen to tear up the roadway. We were proceeding casually along one road when a young officer rode up to us and told us to put on speed because we were under fire from a German battery which daily landed one or two shells in that particular portion of the roadway. It is wonderful how obedient one becomes at times! We promptly proceeded to hasten! After visiting General Debeney and obtaining from him the necessary authorisation and an officer escort, we entered Rheims.

The cathedral is now the home of pigeons, and as they fly in and out of the blackened window-frames small pieces of the stained glass tinkle down on to the floor. The custodian of the cathedral told us that during the night of terror the German wounded, lying in the cathedral, not realising the strength and beauty of the French character under adversity, feared, seeing the cathedral in flames, that the populace might wreak vengeance on them, and that it was exceedingly difficult to get them to leave the cathedral. Many of the prisoners fled into corners and hid, and some of them even penetrated into the palace of the Archbishop, which was in flames. All the world knows and admires the bravery of the cure of the cathedral, M. Landrieux, who took upon himself the defence of the prisoners, for fear insults might be hurled at them. He knowingly risked his life, but when, next day, some of his confreres endeavoured to praise him he replied: "My friends, I never before realised how easy it was to die."

One of the churches in the city was heavily draped in black, and I asked the sacristan if they had prepared for the funeral of a prominent citizen. He told me that they were that day bringing home the body of a young man of high birth of the neighbourhood, but that it was not for him that the church was decked in mourning. The draperies had hung there since August, 1914--"Since every son of Rheims who is brought home is as noble as the one who comes to-day, and alas! nearly every day brings us one of our children."

We lunched in the hotel before the cathedral, where each shell hole has an ordinary white label stuck beside it with the date. The landlord remarked: "If you sit here long enough, and have the good luck to be in some safe part of the building, you may be able to go and stick a label on a hole yourself."

After lunch we went out to the Chateau Polignac. To a stranger it would appear to be almost entirely destroyed, but when M. de Polignac visited it recently he simply remarked that it was "less spoilt than he had imagined." This was just one other example of the thousands one meets daily of the spirit of noble and peasant, "de ne pas s'en faire" but to keep only before them the one idea, Victory for France, no matter what may be the cost.

We went later to call on the "75," chez elle. Madame was in a particularly comfortable home which had been prepared for her and where she was safe from the inquisitive eyes of the Taubes. The men of the battery were sitting round their guns, singing a somewhat lengthy ditty, each verse ending with a declamation and a description of the beauty of "la belle Suzanne." I asked them to whom Suzanne belonged and where the fair damsel resided. "Oh," they replied, "we have no time to think of damsels called 'Suzanne' now. This is our Suzanne," and the speaker affectionately gave an extra rub with his coat sleeve to the barrel of the "75." By a wonderful system of trench work it is possible for the gunners, in case of necessity, to take refuge in the champagne vaults in the surrounding district, and it is in the champagne vaults that the children go daily to school, with their little gas masks hanging in bags on their arms. It appears that at first the tiny ones were frightened of the masks, but they soon asked, like their elders, to be also given a sack, and now one and all have learnt at the least alarm to put on their masks. There is no need to tell the children to hurry home. They realise that it is not wise to loiter in the streets for fear of the whistling shells. They are remarkably plucky, these small men and women of France.

During one furious bombardment the children were safe in the vaults, but one small citizen began to cry bitterly. He was reproached by his comrades for cowardice, but he replied indignantly: "I fear nothing for myself. I am safe here, but there is no cellar to our house, and oh, what will happen to the little mother?" The teacher reassured him by telling him that his mother would certainly take refuge in somebody's else cellar.

On leaving Rheims we passed through various small hamlets where the houses had been entirely destroyed, and which now had the appearance of native villages, as the soldiers had managed to place thatched roofs on any place which had any semblance of walls standing.

At Villars Coterets the Guard Champetre sounded the "Gare a Vous!" Four Taubes were passing overhead, so we took refuge in the hotel for tea. The enemy did no damage in that particular village, but in the next village of Crepy-en-Valois a bomb killed one child and injured five women.

At The Headquarters Of The Generalissimo

At his Headquarters next morning I had the honour of being received by Generalissimo Joffre and telling him of the admiration and respect which we felt for him and for the magnificent fighting spirit of the troops under his able command. He replied modestly by speaking of the British army. He referred to the offensive on the Somme, and said, "You may well be proud of your young soldiers; they are excellent soldiers, much superior to the Germans in every way, a most admirable infantry; they attack the Germans hand to hand with grenades or with the bayonet and push them back everywhere; the Germans have been absolutely stupefied to find such troops before them." The General then paid a tribute to the Canadian and Australian troops and told me that that day the Australians had taken new territory, adding, "And not only have they taken it, but, like their British and Canadian brothers, what they take they will hold."

I explained to General Joffre that, whilst I was not collecting autographs, I had with me the menu of the dinner in the Citadel at Verdun and that it would give me great pleasure to have his name added to the signatures already on that menu. All the signatures were on one side, so I turned the menu over in order to offer him a clear space, but he turned it back again, saying, "Please let me sign on this side. I find myself in good company with the defenders of Verdun."

At departing he said to me, "We may all be happy now since certainly we are on the right side of the hill." ("Nous sommes sur la bonne pente.")

In case this little story should fall into the hands of any woman who has spent her time working for the men at the Front, I would like to tell her the great pleasure it is to them to receive parcels, no matter what they contain. Fraternity and Equality reign supreme in the trenches, and the man counts himself happy who receives a little more than the others, since he has the joy and the pleasure of sharing his store of good things with his comrades. There is seldom a request made to the French behind the lines that they do not attempt to fulfil. I remember last winter, passing through a town in the provinces, I noticed that the elderly men appeared to be scantily clad in spite of the bitterness of the weather. It appeared that the call had gone forth for fur coats for the troops, and all the worthy citizens of the town forwarded to the trenches their caracul coats. Only those who are well acquainted with French provincial life can know what it means to them to part with these signs of opulence and commercial success.

It is perhaps in the Post Offices that you find yourself nearest to the heart of "France behind the lines."

One morning I endeavoured to send a parcel to a French soldier. I took my place in a long line of waiting women bound on the same errand. A white-haired woman before me gave the Post Office Clerk infinite trouble. They are not re-nowned for their patience and I marvelled at his gentleness until he explained. "Her son died five weeks ago, but she still continues to send him parcels."

To another old lady he pointed out that she had written two numbers on the parcel. "You don't want two numbers, Mother. Which is your boy's number? Tell me and I will strike out the other." "Leave them both," she answered. "Who knows whether my dear lad will be there to receive the parcel. If he is not, I want it to go to some other Mother's son."

Affection means much to these men who are suffering, and they respond at once to any sympathy shown to them. One man informed us with pride that when he left his native village he was "decked like an altar of the Blessed Virgin on the first of May." In other words, covered with flowers.

There are but few lonely soldiers now, since those who have no families to write to them receive letters and parcels from the Godmothers who have adopted them. The men anxiously await the news of their adopted relatives and spend hours writing replies. They love to receive letters, but, needless to say, a parcel is even more welcome.

I remember seeing one man writing page after page. I suggested to him that he must have a particularly charming Godmother. "Mademoiselle," he replied, "I have no time for a Godmother since I myself am a Godfather." He then explained that far away in his village there was a young assistant in his shop, "And God knows the boy loves France, but both his lungs are touched, so they won't take him, but I write and tell him that the good God has given me strength for two, that I fight for him and for myself, and that we are both doing well for France." I went back in imagination to the village. I could see the glint in the boy's eyes, realised how the blood pulsed quicker through his veins at the sight of, not the personal pronoun "I" in the singular, but the plural "We are doing well for France." For one glorious moment he was part of the hosts of France and in spirit serving his Motherland. It is that spirit of the French nation that their enemies will never understand.

On one occasion a young German officer, covered with mud from head to foot, was brought before one of the French Generals. He had been taken fighting cleanly, and the General was anxious to show him kindness. He asked him if he would not prefer to cleanse himself before examination. The young German drew himself up and replied: "Look at me, General. I am covered from head to foot with mud, and that mud is the soil of France--you will never possess as much soil in Germany." The General turned to him with that gentle courtesy which marks the higher commands in France and answered: "Monsieur, we may never possess as much soil in Germany, but there is something that you will never possess, and, until you conquer it, you cannot vanquish France, and that is the spirit of the French people."

The French find it difficult to understand the arrogance which appears ingrained in the German character and which existed before the War.

I read once that in the guests' book of a French hotel a Teutonic visitor wrote:

"L'Allemagne est la premiere nation du monde."

The next French visitor merely added:

"Yes, 'Allemagne is the first country of the world' if we take them in alphabetical order."

To The Glory Of The Women Of France

I left the war zone with an increased respect, if this were possible, for the men of France. They have altered their uniforms, but the spirit is unchanged. They are no longer in the red and blue of the old days, but in shades of green, grey and blue, colours blending to form one mighty ocean--wave on wave of patriotism--beating against and wearing down the rocks of military preparedness of forty years, and as no man has yet been able to say to the Ocean stop, so no man shall cry "Halt" to the Armies of France.

I have spoken much of the men of France, but the women have also earned our respect--those splendid peasant women, who even in times of peace worked, and now carry a double burden on their shoulders--the middle-class women, endeavouring to keep together the little business built up by the man with years of toil, stinting themselves to save five francs to send a parcel to the man at the Front that he may not suspect that there is not still every comfort in the little homestead--the noble women of France, who in past years could not be seen before noon, since my lady was at her toilette, and who can be seen now, their hands scratched and bleeding, kneeling on the floors of the hospitals scrubbing, proud and happy to take their part in national service. The men owe much of their courage to the attitude of the women who stand behind them, turning their tears to smiles to urge their men to even greater deeds of heroism.

In one of our hospitals was a young lad of seventeen who had managed to enlist as an "engage volontaire" by lying as to his age. His old Mother came to visit him, and she told me he was the last of her three sons; the two elder ones had died the first week of the war at Pont Mousson, and her little home had been burned to the ground. The boy had spent his time inventing new and terrible methods of dealing with the enemy, but with his Mother he became a child again and tenderly patted the old face. Seeing the lad in his Mother's arms, and forgetting for one moment the spirit of the French nation, I asked her if she would not be glad if her boy was so wounded that she might take him home. She was only an old peasant woman, but her eyes flashed, her cheeks flushed with anger and turning to me she said, "Mademoiselle, how dare you say such a thing to me? If all the Mothers, Wives and Sweethearts thought as you, what would happen to the country? Gustave has only one thing to do, get well quickly and fight for Mother France."

Because these women of France have sent their men forth to die, eyes dry, with stiff lips and head erect, do not think that they do not mourn for them. When night casts her kindly mantle of darkness over all, when they are hidden from the eyes of the world, it is then that the proud heads droop and are bent upon their arms, as the women cry out in the bitterness of their souls for the men who have gone from them. Yet they realise that behind them stands the greatest Mother of all, Mother France, who sees coming towards her, from her frontiers, line on line of ambulances with their burden of suffering humanity, yet watches along other routes her sons going forth in thousands, laughter in their eyes, songs on their lips, ready and willing to die for her. France draws around her her tattered and bloodstained robe, yet what matters the outer raiment? Behind it shines forth her glorious, exultant soul, and she lifts up her head rejoicing and proclaims to the world that when she appealed man, woman, and child--the whole of the French nation-- answered to her call.

The Codes Of Hammurabi And Moses
W. W. Davies

The discovery of the Hammurabi Code is one of the greatest achievements of archaeology, and is of paramount interest, not only to the student of the Bible, but also to all those interested in ancient history...

Religion   **ISBN:** *1-59462-338-4*

QTY

Pages:132
MSRP $12.95

The Theory of Moral Sentiments
Adam Smith

This work from 1749. contains original theories of conscience amd moral judgment and it is the foundation for systemof morals.

Philosophy   ISBN: *1-59462-777-0*

QTY

Pages:536
MSRP $19.95

Jessica's First Prayer
Hesba Stretton

In a screened and secluded corner of one of the many railway-bridges which span the streets of London there could be seen a few years ago, from five o'clock every morning until half past eight, a tidily set-out coffee-stall, consisting of a trestle and board, upon which stood two large tin cans, with a small fire of charcoal burning under each so as to keep the coffee boiling during the early hours of the morning when the work-people were thronging into the city on their way to their daily toil...

Childrens   ISBN: *1-59462-373-2*

QTY

Pages:84
MSRP $9.95

My Life and Work
Henry Ford

Henry Ford revolutionized the world with his implementation of mass production for the Model T automobile. Gain valuable business insight into his life and work with his own auto-biography... "We have only started on our development of our country we have not as yet, with all our talk of wonderful progress, done more than scratch the surface. The progress has been wonderful enough but..."

Biographies/   **ISBN:** *1-59462-198-5*

QTY

Pages:300
MSRP $21.95

The Art of Cross-Examination
Francis Wellman

QTY

I presume it is the experience of every author, after his first book is published upon an important subject, to be almost overwhelmed with a wealth of ideas and illustrations which could readily have been included in his book, and which to his own mind, at least, seem to make a second edition inevitable. Such certainly was the case with me; and when the first edition had reached its sixth impression in five months, I rejoiced to learn that it seemed to my publishers that the book had met with a sufficiently favorable reception to justify a second and considerably enlarged edition. ..

Pages:412

Reference   **ISBN: *1-59462-647-2***   *MSRP $19.95*

On the Duty of Civil Disobedience
Henry David Thoreau

QTY

Thoreau wrote his famous essay, On the Duty of Civil Disobedience, as a protest against an unjust but popular war and the immoral but popular institution of slave-owning. He did more than write—he declined to pay his taxes, and was hauled off to gaol in consequence. Who can say how much this refusal of his hastened the end of the war and of slavery ?

Law   **ISBN: *1-59462-747-9***   **Pages:48**

MSRP $7.45

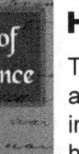

Dream Psychology Psychoanalysis for Beginners
Sigmund Freud

QTY

Sigmund Freud, born Sigismund Schlomo Freud (May 6, 1856 - September 23, 1939), was a Jewish-Austrian neurologist and psychiatrist who co-founded the psychoanalytic school of psychology. Freud is best known for his theories of the unconscious mind, especially involving the mechanism of repression; his redefinition of sexual desire as mobile and directed towards a wide variety of objects; and his therapeutic techniques, especially his understanding of transference in the therapeutic relationship and the presumed value of dreams as sources of insight into unconscious desires.

Pages:196

Psychology   **ISBN: *1-59462-905-6***   *MSRP $15.45*

Dream Psychology
Psychoanalysis for Beginners

Sigmund Freud

The Miracle of Right Thought
Orison Swett Marden

QTY

Believe with all of your heart that you will do what you were made to do. When the mind has once formed the habit of holding cheerful, happy, prosperous pictures, it will not be easy to form the opposite habit. It does not matter how improbable or how far away this realization may see, or how dark the prospects may be, if we visualize them as best we can, as vividly as possible, hold tenaciously to them and vigorously struggle to attain them, they will gradually become actualized, realized in the life. But a desire, a longing without endeavor, a yearning abandoned or held indifferently will vanish without realization.

Pages:360

Self Help   **ISBN: *1-59462-644-8***   *MSRP $25.45*

QTY

☐ **The Rosicrucian Cosmo-Conception Mystic Christianity** *by Max Heindel*   ISBN: *1-59462-188-8*   **$38.95**
The Rosicrucian Cosmo-conception is not dogmatic, neither does it appeal to any other authority than the reason of the student. It is: not controversial, but is: sent forth in the, hope that it may help to clear...   New Age/Religion Pages 646

☐ **Abandonment To Divine Providence** *by Jean-Pierre de Caussade*   ISBN: *1-59462-228-0*   **$25.95**
"The Rev. Jean Pierre de Caussade was one of the most remarkable spiritual writers of the Society of Jesus in France in the 18th Century. His death took place at Toulouse in 1751. His works have gone through many editions and have been republished...   Inspirational/Religion Pages 400

☐ **Mental Chemistry** *by Charles Haanel*   ISBN: *1-59462-192-6*   **$23.95**
Mental Chemistry allows the change of material conditions by combining and appropriately utilizing the power of the mind. Much like applied chemistry creates something new and unique out of careful combinations of chemicals the mastery of mental chemistry...   New Age Pages 354

☐ **The Letters of Robert Browning and Elizabeth Barret Barrett 1845-1846 vol II**   ISBN: *1-59462-193-4*   **$35.95**
by Robert Browning and Elizabeth Barrett   Biographies Pages 596

☐ **Gleanings In Genesis (volume I)** *by Arthur W. Pink*   ISBN: *1-59462-130-6*   **$27.45**
Appropriately has Genesis been termed "the seed plot of the Bible" for in it we have, in germ form, almost all of the great doctrines which are afterwards fully developed in the books of Scripture which follow...   Religion/Inspirational Pages 420

☐ **The Master Key** *by L. W. de Laurence*   ISBN: *1-59462-001-6*   **$30.95**
In no branch of human knowledge has there been a more lively increase of the spirit of research during the past few years than in the study of Psychology, Concentration and Mental Discipline. The requests for authentic lessons in Thought Control, Mental Discipline and...   New Age/Business Pages 422

☐ **The Lesser Key Of Solomon Goetia** *by L. W. de Laurence*   ISBN: *1-59462-092-X*   **$9.95**
This translation of the first book of the "Lernegton" which is now for the first time made accessible to students of Talismanic Magic was done, after careful collation and edition, from numerous Ancient Manuscripts in Hebrew, Latin, and French...   New Age/Occult Pages 92

☐ **Rubaiyat Of Omar Khayyam** *by Edward Fitzgerald*   ISBN: *1-59462-332-5*   **$13.95**
Edward Fitzgerald, whom the world has already learned, in spite of his own efforts to remain within the shadow of anonymity, to look upon as one of the rarest poets of the century, was born at Bredfield, in Suffolk, on the 31st of March, 1809. He was the third son of John Purcell...   Music Pages 172

☐ **Ancient Law** *by Henry Maine*   ISBN: *1-59462-128-4*   **$29.95**
The chief object of the following pages is to indicate some of the earliest ideas of mankind, as they are reflected in Ancient Law, and to point out the relation of those ideas to modern thought.   Religion/History Pages 452

☐ **Far-Away Stories** *by William J. Locke*   ISBN: *1-59462-129-2*   **$19.45**
"Good wine needs no bush, but a collection of mixed vintages does. And this book is just such a collection. Some of the stories I do not want to remain buried for ever in the museum files of dead magazine-numbers an author's not unpardonable vanity..."   Fiction Pages 272

☐ **Life of David Crockett** *by David Crockett*   ISBN: *1-59462-250-7*   **$27.45**
"Colonel David Crockett was one of the most remarkable men of the times in which he lived. Born in humble life, but gifted with a strong will, an indomitable courage, and unremitting perseverance...   Biographies/New Age Pages 424

☐ **Lip-Reading** *by Edward Nitchie*   ISBN: *1-59462-206-X*   **$25.95**
Edward B. Nitchie, founder of the New York School for the Hard of Hearing, now the Nitchie School of Lip-Reading, Inc, wrote "LIP-READING Principles and Practice". The development and perfecting of this meritorious work on lip-reading was an undertaking...   How-to Pages 400

☐ **A Handbook of Suggestive Therapeutics, Applied Hypnotism, Psychic Science**   ISBN: *1-59462-214-0*   **$24.95**
by Henry Munro   Health/New Age/Health/Self-help Pages 376

☐ **A Doll's House: and Two Other Plays** *by Henrik Ibsen*   ISBN: *1-59462-112-8*   **$19.95**
Henrik Ibsen created this classic when in revolutionary 1848 Rome. Introducing some striking concepts in playwriting for the realist genre, this play has been studied the world over.   Fiction/Classics/Plays 308

☐ **The Light of Asia** *by sir Edwin Arnold*   ISBN: *1-59462-204-3*   **$13.95**
In this poetic masterpiece, Edwin Arnold describes the life and teachings of Buddha. The man who was to become known as Buddha to the world was born as Prince Gautama of India but he rejected the worldly riches and abandoned the reigns of power when...   Religion/History/Biographies Pages 170

☐ **The Complete Works of Guy de Maupassant** *by Guy de Maupassant*   ISBN: *1-59462-157-8*   **$16.95**
"For days and days, nights and nights, I had dreamed of that first kiss which was to consecrate our engagement, and I knew not on what spot I should put my lips..."   Fiction/Classics Pages 240

☐ **The Art of Cross-Examination** *by Francis L. Wellman*   ISBN: *1-59462-309-0*   **$26.95**
Written by a renowned trial lawyer, Wellman imparts his experience and uses case studies to explain how to use psychology to extract desired information through questioning.   How-to/Science/Reference Pages 408

☐ **Answered or Unanswered?** *by Louisa Vaughan*   ISBN: *1-59462-248-5*   **$10.95**
Miracles of Faith in China   Religion Pages 112

☐ **The Edinburgh Lectures on Mental Science (1909)** *by Thomas*   ISBN: *1-59462-008-3*   **$11.95**
This book contains the substance of a course of lectures recently given by the writer in the Queen Street Hail, Edinburgh. Its purpose is to indicate the Natural Principles governing the relation between Mental Action and Material Conditions...   New Age/Psychology Pages 148

☐ **Ayesha** *by H. Rider Haggard*   ISBN: *1-59462-301-5*   **$24.95**
Verily and indeed it is the unexpected that happens! Probably if there was one person upon the earth from whom the Editor of this, and of a certain previous history, did not expect to hear again...   Classics Pages 380

☐ **Ayala's Angel** *by Anthony Trollope*   ISBN: *1-59462-352-X*   **$29.95**
The two girls were both pretty, but Lucy who was twenty-one who supposed to be simple and comparatively unattractive, whereas Ayala was credited, as her Bombwhat romantic name might show, with poetic charm and a taste for romance. Ayala when her father died was nineteen...   Fiction Pages 484

☐ **The American Commonwealth** *by James Bryce*   ISBN: *1-59462-286-8*   **$34.45**
An interpretation of American democratic political theory. It examines political mechanics and society from the perspective of Scotsman James Bryce   Politics Pages 572

☐ **Stories of the Pilgrims** *by Margaret P. Pumphrey*   ISBN: *1-59462-116-0*   **$17.95**
This book explores pilgrims religious oppression in England as well as their escape to Holland and eventual crossing to America on the Mayflower, and their early days in New England...   History Pages 268

QTY

The Fasting Cure *by Sinclair Upton*   ISBN: *1-59462-222-1*   **$13.95**
In the Cosmopolitan Magazine for May, 1910, and in the Contemporary Review (London) for April, 1910, I published an article dealing with my experiences in fasting. I have written a great many magazine articles, but never one which attracted so much attention... New Age/Self Help/Health Pages 164

Hebrew Astrology *by Sepharial*   ISBN: *1-59462-308-2*   **$13.45**
In these days of advanced thinking it is a matter of common observation that we have left many of the old landmarks behind and that we are now pressing forward to greater heights and to a wider horizon than that which represented the mind-content of our progenitors... Astrology Pages 144

Thought Vibration or The Law of Attraction in the Thought World   ISBN: *1-59462-127-6*   **$12.95**
by William Walker Atkinson   Psychology/Religion Pages 144

Optimism *by Helen Keller*   ISBN: *1-59462-108-X*   **$15.95**
Helen Keller was blind, deaf, and mute since 19 months old, yet famously learned how to overcome these handicaps, communicate with the world, and spread her lectures promoting optimism. An inspiring read for everyone... Biographies/Inspirational Pages 84

Sara Crewe *by Frances Burnett*   ISBN: *1-59462-360-0*   **$9.45**
In the first place, Miss Minchin lived in London. Her home was a large, dull, tall one, in a large, dull square, where all the houses were alike, and all the sparrows were alike, and where all the door-knockers made the same heavy sound... Childrens/Classic Pages 88

The Autobiography of Benjamin Franklin *by Benjamin Franklin*   ISBN: *1-59462-135-7*   **$24.95**
The Autobiography of Benjamin Franklin has probably been more extensively read than any other American historical work, and no other book of its kind has had such ups and downs of fortune. Franklin lived for many years in England, where he was agent... Biographies/History Pages 332

Name	
Email	
Telephone	
Address	
City, State ZIP	

☐ **Credit Card**   ☐ **Check / Money Order**

Credit Card Number	
Expiration Date	
Signature	

Please Mail to: Book Jungle
                    PO Box 2226
                    Champaign, IL 61825
or Fax to: 630-214-0564

ORDERING INFORMATION

web: *www.bookjungle.com*
email: *sales@bookjungle.com*
fax: *630-214-0564*
mail: *Book Jungle PO Box 2226 Champaign, IL 61825*
or PayPal *to sales@bookjungle.com*

Please contact us for bulk discounts

DIRECT-ORDER TERMS

**20% Discount if You Order
Two or More Books**
Free Domestic Shipping!
Accepted: Master Card, Visa,
Discover, American Express

www.ingramcontent.com/pod-product-compliance
Lightning Source LLC
Chambersburg PA
CBHW081306200626
46813CB00018B/3277